P9-BZJ-088

THE
SNOW DAY
FROM THE
BLACK LAGOON

THE
SNOW DAY
FROM THE
BLACK LAGOON

by Mike Thaler
Illustrated by Jared Lee

SCHOLASTIC INC.

New York   Toronto   London   Auckland   Sydney
Mexico City   New Delhi   Hong Kong   Buenos Aires

To
Akimi & Janelle
Creative Partners—M.T.

To my big brother, Jim,
who is always calm, cool, and collected—J.L.

No part of this publication may be reproduced, stored in a retrieval system, or transmitted in any form or by any means, electronic, mechanical, photocopying, recording, or otherwise, without written permission of the publisher. For information regarding permission, write to Scholastic Inc., Attention: Permissions Department, 557 Broadway, New York, NY 10012.

ISBN-13: 978-0-545-01766-4
ISBN-10: 0-545-01766-1

Text copyright © 2008 by Mike Thaler.
Illustrations copyright © 2008 by Jared D. Lee Studio, Inc.

All rights reserved. Published by Scholastic Inc.

SCHOLASTIC, LITTLE APPLE, and associated logos are trademarks and/or registered trademarks of Scholastic Inc.

29 28   18 19/0

Printed in the U.S.A.
First printing, February 2008

CONTENTS

CHAPTER 1
THERE'S NO BUSINESS LIKE SNOW BUSINESS

I hate winter! Winter should last for one day right before Christmas.

And snow…I hate snow. There should be just enough to powder the corners of windows, like in greeting cards. But instead, winter lasts for months and months and the snow piles up until everything is buried underneath it.

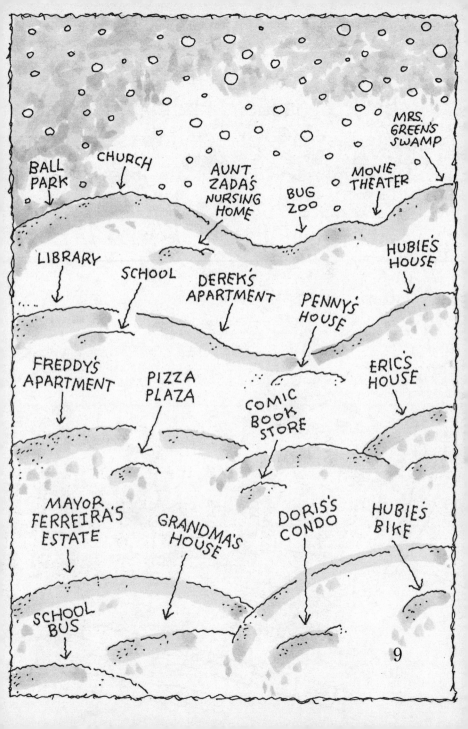

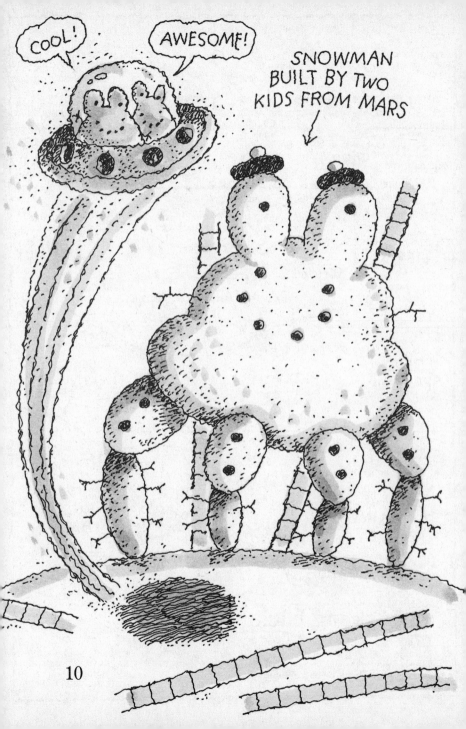

10

CHAPTER 2
DRESSED TO THE TEETH

And the clothes you have to wear to go outside—you're buried in layers of itchy wool. You spend half the day zipping up zippers, snapping snaps, and buckling buckles.

Then there's the mile-long scarf your aunt knits for you that you have to wrap around and around. And don't forget the rubber overshoes that totally resist going over shoes.

BUG EATER →

12

Last but not least, there's the wool cap, earmuffs, and mittens that cover up every last bit of you.

REMOVABLE BALL

ADJUSTABLE

THE DELUXE MODEL COMES WITH A MINI RADIO

TIGHT RUBBER OVERSHOES

WATERPROOF BUT NOT SNOWPROOF

Now you're a proper mummy, ready to be buried in the white tomb of winter.

MUMMY→

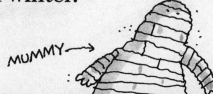

And just when you get everything zipped, snapped, and buckled, you have to go to the bathroom, which means starting all over again. So by the time you're ready to go outside…it's dark. That's another thing— during the winter, the sun goes on vacation to Florida, and daylight only lasts for a couple of hours. I hate winter!

HUBIE, DO YOU NEED TO GO TO THE BATHROOM?

MAYBE.

15

EXACT SIZE ←

CHAPTER 3
THE BLIZZARD OF OZ

So when I turn on the weather channel and see a winter blizzard warning for my area, I get very nervous. And when I hear that two to three feet of snow is expected, I really panic. That doesn't mean a snow day, it means a no day—nothing moves, nothing happens.

SMELLS GOOD!

DON'T EAT ME.

ENGLISH

17

Your house becomes an igloo and your town becomes the tundra. Your life is frozen like a TV dinner. If you could have a snow day when the sun is shining and you could get out of your front door, that would be one thing. But a snow day that's full of snow is another.

TV DINNER INSTRUCTIONS; POKE HOLES THROUGH PLASTIC FILM SO THAT HUBIE AND HIS DOG CAN BREATHE. PLACE IN MICROWAVE FOR THREE MINUTES, THEN STIR UNTIL WAKENED.

Eric calls. He's all excited. He talks like the circus is coming to town instead of a blizzard.

21

"Come on, Hubie. There's so much we can do!" he says.

"Like what?" I ask.

"Winter sports," he answers.

"You mean like shoveling out the driveway and slipping on the ice?"

"No, like sledding and ice skating and skiing," he explains. "It'll be great!"

"I like my sports played on reliable surfaces—solid, non-skid surfaces."

"Boy," sighs Eric, "you don't know what fun is!"

25

CHAPTER 5
THE ARCTIC IS FOR THE BYRDS

That night it snows. It always amazes me how those pretty little flakes can quietly turn into a great white monster by morning.

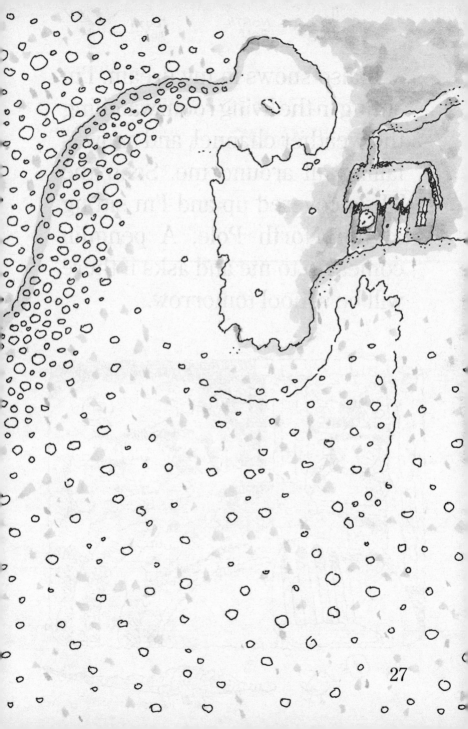

It also snows in my dream. I'm sitting in the living room watching the weather channel, and snow is falling all around me. Soon the TV is covered up and I'm sitting at the North Pole. A penguin comes up to me and asks if there will be school tomorrow.

"I don't think so," I say. "How are the roads?"

"Icy," says the penguin.

"You see what?" I ask.

"Icy, icy," says the penguin.

"I know you see, but how are the roads?"

The penguin doesn't answer.

CHAPTER 6
COLD TURKEY

I think I'll stay in bed all day. It's warm and dry and safe. But mom comes bounding in just as I'm snuggling down.

"Come on, Hubie. It's beautiful outside. It snowed all night."

"Mom, I know."

"Let's get dressed, go out, and make a snowman!"

Uh-oh, I know what that means. Sixteen layers of mittens, hats, scarves, hoods, boots, pants, sweaters...

"Come on, Hubie. You'll love it."

I won't love it. But I love Mom, so I'll humor her. I start by putting on my thermal underwear and build from there. Around noon, I button the last button and snap the last snap.

33

"Mom, I'm hungry."

"Okay, Hubie, let's have lunch. Open up your snowsuit a little so you won't get overheated."

So I unzip and unsnap and have lunch. After lunch, I'm back on the launch pad. All systems go...

10, 9, 8, 7, 6, 5, 4, 3, 2, 1...

BLAST OUT!

WHAT YOU CAN USE FOR THE SNOWMAN'S NOSE INSTEAD OF A CARROT.

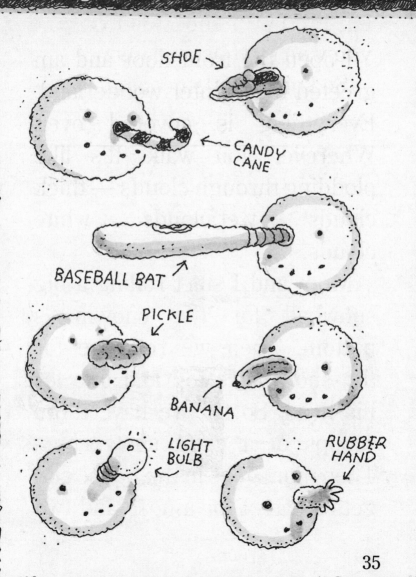

SHOE

CANDY CANE

BASEBALL BAT

PICKLE

BANANA

LIGHT BULB

RUBBER HAND

CHAPTER 7
ARCTIC EXPEDITION

I open the front door and am greeted by a winter wonderland. Everything is covered over. Wherever you walk, it's like plodding through clouds — thick clouds . . . wet clouds . . . white clouds.

Mom and I start rolling a big snowball for the snowman's bottom. Then we roll one for the snowman's top and one for his head. So far, we have three scoops of a giant snow cone. Then mom goes in the house and gets a carrot for a nose and two

CLOUD →

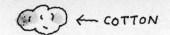

radishes for eyes. I put my cap on him and I must say, he looks pretty impressive.

Eric comes over with his sled and we tramp off to find a hill. The closest we come to one is my neighbor's driveway. So we pile on the sled and let it rip! Fun!

39

After thirty rides, we build a snow fort and have a snowball fight with Freddy and Derek who have wandered over.

I DON'T DO PERKY.

CHAPTER 8
PERKS

After a truce has been declared, we go inside. Mom gives us hot apple cider and we all dry off. I take out one of my board games and we're good for another two hours. It starts to snow again so Mom says that Freddy, Eric, and Derek can stay over. Mom builds a fire in the fireplace and we all toast marshmallows and tell ghost stories.

SOMETHING DOESN'T LOOK RIGHT.

43

DEREK'S SCARY GHOST STORY

SAMMY WAS A LONELY GHOST.

HE HAD NOBODY TO SCARE.

HE PUT A HELP WANTED AD IN THE NEWSPAPER.

I CAN SCARE THEM ON THE PHONE.

NO ONE CALLED.

44

TOASTED MARSHMALLOW →

I LIKE THIS STORY.

45

ERIC →

CHAPTER 9
WINTER TALES

Eric tells us the story of the Killer Snowman.

"There were these people who made a snowman with a carrot nose and radish eyes. It sat on their front lawn and didn't move...until it was struck by lightning. Then it blinked its radish eyes, blew its carrot nose, and started to walk like Frankenstein."

← BLACK CLOUD

"Why didn't it melt?" asks Freddy.

"What melt?"

"The snowman—when it was hit by lightning."

"It didn't melt—it came to life."

"It would have melted."

"This is my story," says Eric.

"Anyway, it came to life and went looking for an ice-cream store."

"Why?" asks Derek.

"Because it was hungry," answers Eric.

"What did it eat?" I asked.

"A snow cone," says Eric.

I look out the window and our snowman is still standing quietly in the moonlight.

Suddenly, there's a knock at the door. We all freeze.

CHAPTER 10
GO FOR THE GOLD

It's our neighbor with his snow blower. He offers to clear our driveway.

"That's okay," says Mom. "It's nice to be snowed in."

It's true. We were all stranded on a fireplace island in a sea of snow. After hot chocolate and more ghost stories, we go to bed.

I have a funny dream that night. I'm in the winter Olympics. I'm entered in every event—skiing, ski jumping, speed skating, even bobsledding. I am fantastic and

← HOT COCOA

51

win 21 gold medals. In figure skating, my partner is the snowman. But he melts before we can finish our routine.

I'm awakened by the sound of the snowplows clearing our street. That means that there will be school today.

THREE BEARS AND A PIG

CHAPTER 11
A SCHOOL DAY

The school bus picks us up at the usual time. We all sit bundled up in stocking caps and earmuffs. The bus smells like wet wool.

At school, Fester has turned the radiators up to full steam and the classrooms are toasty.

Mrs. Green asks us to write a report about what we did on our snow day. This is my report, and I must admit I did have a good time. I still don't like winter, but it would be okay if it lasted for a week...if every day of that week was a snow day.

58

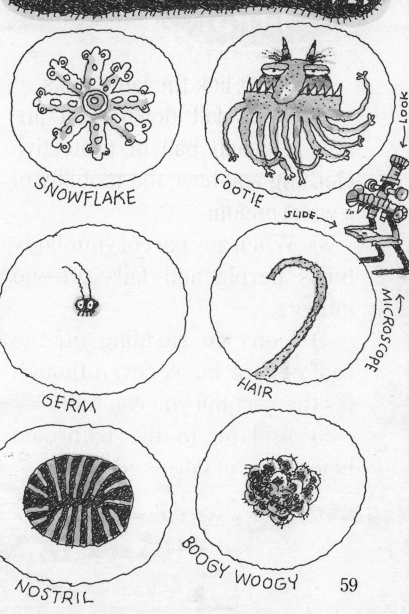

1) Don't lick the lampposts.

2) Don't fall down. You are now a beach ball of protective clothing and have the mobility of a watermelon.

3) When any part of your body turns purple and falls off—go indoors.

4) Don't go sledding off the roof of your house, even though it's the best hill you can find.

5) And go to the bathroom <u>before</u> you get dressed.

61

SNOW DAY JOKES

WHAT DO YOU CALL A FROZEN RODENT?

I CAN'T MOVE.

A MICECICLE.

WHAT DO YOU CALL A BABY CAT'S GLOVES?

MEOW.

A KITTEN'S MITTENS.

WHAT DO ESKIMOS STICK THEIR HOUSES TOGETHER WITH?

MOM, IT'S COLD IN HERE.

CLOSE YOUR WINDOW.

IGLOO

WHAT'S THE COLDEST COUNTRY?

TURN UP THE HEAT!

CHILE

WHY IS AN ICE CUBE SO SMART?

ASK ME ANYTHING.

BECAUSE IT HAS 32 DEGREES.

WHAT DO YOU CALL SNOWSTORMS CAUSED BY A MAGICIAN?

A WIZARD'S BLIZZARDS.

63